Written by Marco Arana.

First edition. August 5, 2024.

ISBN: 9798224786893

ONE MILLION
IDEAS
STORE
MARCO ARANA

A Story for Kids

Sofia's story is charming and full of imagination. The way she describes her adventures is very colorful, allowing readers to feel the excitement and joy of being kids. Her friends, Silfo and Silfides, add a magical and mysterious touch, and the idea of a key that opens the door to dreams is a fascinating concept that invites exploration.

The transition to the world of Air Elementals is very creative and teaches a valuable lesson about the power of thoughts and imagination. It's great how elements of fantasy are mixed with lessons. The story not only entertains but also leaves an important message for young readers. Overall, it's a magical tale that combines adventure, friendship, and learning in a very appealing way. It's definitely a story that many kids will enjoy and remember!

"The Journey of Sofia"

A sunny Saturday

The Excitement for
a New Day
**The anticipation of a day
full of possibilities**

It was a sunny Saturday and Sofía woke up full of excitement. She looked out the window and saw that the sky was clear, with a few fluffy clouds that seemed to invite her to come out and play.

Preparations for Adventure

A New Day, A New Challenges

The importance of being ready
and excited for new experiences.

After a yummy breakfast, Sofia ran to her room and put on her favorite clothes: a flowered dress and comfortable sandals. I was ready for a day full of adventures.

The Park of Joy

Collective Joy
The happiness found in community and play.

He decided to visit the park near his house. Upon arrival, he found an atmosphere full of joy and life. The children ran across the grass, laughing out loud and having fun on the swings and slides.

New Friends in the Park

Friendship and Energy
The connection that is formed through fun and shared adventure

Sofía, excited by the energy of the place, headed towards an area where two children, a boy and a girl, were playing happily. The boy, with blonde hair and blue eyes, was called Silfo. He was an adventurous and playful child, always willing to explore new places and games.

The Sweet Sylphides

Diversity in Friendship
The beauty of meeting people
with different personalities

The girl, with light yellow hair and almond-shaped blue eyes, was called Silfides. She was a sweet and loving girl, who loved socializing and meeting other children.

Constructing dreams

Imagination and creativity
The power of symbolic play and the creation of imaginary worlds

Sofia, along with her new friends, built a dollhouse with branches and leaves, and then they pretended to be princesses and princes of a kingdom where there were many hidden treasures. They ran back and forth, laughing loudly as they chased and hid.

The Magic Key

Friendship Gifts
Generosity and the value of symbolic gifts

Already tired, they sat under a large tree with a protective shade. The children, amazed by Sofia's kindness and innocent spirit, gave her a mysterious magic key that opened the door to dreams, a place where anything was possible.

A special gift

Mystery and Magic
The emotion of receiving
something magical and special

Sofia, excited by the possibility of visiting such a fantastic place, thanked him for the priceless gift. Silfo and Silfides only indicated to Sofía that the key's magic would only work as long as no one found out about its existence.

Mom's Snack

Nutrition and Care
The importance of family and care in special moments.

Quickly, Sofia put the key in her pocket and hid it to keep her promise. At noon, Sofia's stomach began to growl, and she went home, where her mother had a delicious snack for her: peanut butter and jelly sandwiches, fresh fruit, and grape juice.

Transmit stories and adventures

Share experiences

The joy of telling stories and sharing experiences with loved ones

Sofia told her mother about all the adventures she had had during the morning with her new friends. Finally, tired and with a full stomach, it was time to go take a well-deserved nap, feeling exhausted but happy.

Dreams and Memories

Refuge in Dreams
The comfort found in friendship and hope

It had been a wonderful morning, full of games, friendships and fun. Sofia remembered the key they gave her and placed it next to her heart. He curled up in his bed with the faith that he would see his friends again and surrendered to sleep.

The Shining Tunnel

Facing Fear
The insecurity that can arise in the face of the unknown

As she fell asleep, Sofia saw a large tunnel with a very bright light at the end. There was a white door and when he reached it, his heart began to fill with insecurity because he did not know how to enter.

The Voice of Trust

Listening to Intuition
The importance of following inner voices in times of doubt

As the fear grew, the sun, which was bright, began to be obscured by gray clouds. At that moment, he heard a familiar voice that told him:—Use the key.

The Magic Door

Discovery and Adventure
The excitement of entering a new world full of wonders.

Quickly, she found the key she had in her bag, took it out and opened the door. When he passed the threshold of the door, he found himself in a lush forest, illuminated by a soft, magical light.

Forest Secrets

Natural Curiosity
The innate desire to explore and discover the unknown

The trees, tall and majestic, whispered secrets in the wind, and the vibrantly colored flowers gave off an intoxicating aroma. Sofia, feeling an irresistible curiosity, entered the forest, following a path that seemed to shine with its own light.

The Reunion of Friends

Reunion and Joy
The happiness of meeting friends
on special moments.

On her way, Sofía met her friends Silfo and Silfides, who came to receive her. Joy spread to the three of them at their reunion.

A New Reality

Amazement and Questions
The curiosity that awakens the extraordinary in life.

When the excitement of the reunion passed, Sofia saw something strange: her friends had wings like fairies. He immediately asked them:—Sylph, Sylphides, why do you have wings?

The Elementals of Air

Purpose and Service
The value of knowing the purpose behind our actions

—Sylphides and I are Elementals of Air and Wind. God created us to serve human beings in their evolutionary path.

Fantastic creatures

Wonders of nature
The beauty and magic that reside in the natural world

Along the way, Sofia met fantastic creatures: mischievous fairies fluttering among the flowers, playful elves hiding treasures among the roots of the trees, and majestic unicorns galloping gracefully through the forest glade.

Adventure Stories

Learning Through Conversations

The value of listening and learning from the experiences of others

Sofía talked with Silfo and Silfides, listening to their stories and adventures. As I progressed, the forest transformed into increasingly impressive landscapes.

Exploring Wonders

Exploration and Discovery
The joy of discovering new places
and wonders.

He traversed sun-drenched golden meadows, climbed towering mountains with peaks that touched the clouds, and navigated crystalline rivers that reflected the beauty of the sky. In each place she visited, Sofía, along with her new friends, discovered new wonders.

The Shining Castle

Magic in Every Corner
The magic found in special places

Finally, they arrived at a majestic castle located on the top of a hill. The castle shone with an intense light and emanated a magical energy that filled her with joy.

The Golden Gates

Knowledge and Wisdom
The importance of mind and understanding in our life

Sofia, without hesitation, approached the castle and crossed the large golden doors that said: "Everything is Mind." Inside the castle, Sofia was received by the three regents of that kingdom: Pavana, Hichuara and Paralda.

The Study Hall

Beauty and Learning
Admiration for knowledge and beauty in learning

Sofia was very impressed with such beauty. Her hosts invited Sofía to go to their study room, where all the information about the Elementals of Air and Wind was found, and they put Silfo and Sylfides at her disposal to guide her with any concerns.

Sofia's Experience

Consciousness and Dreams
Reflection on the nature of reality and dreams

Sofia, as she was aware that she was asleep and that her physical body was somewhere else, wanted to know how all that experience she was living was possible.

The Great Higher Being

The Interconnection
The understanding that everything is connected in one big dream.

—When you are in the physical world and you look around you, at the trees, animals and stars, you cannot imagine that everything you observe is part of the dream of a great superior being who has a very powerful mind.

The Architect of the Universe

The Creator of the Universe
The recognition of a higher force behind existence

This mind is from the great architect of the universe, a spirit that has created everything we know. Although we cannot see it, it is behind everything that exists.

Your Inner World

The power of imagination
The ability to dream and create realities in our minds

Your mind is also a small world that can create everything you dream of. Observe this dream here: you can fly, talk to animals or visit magical places. Even though it's a dream, it feels very real, right?

The Universe like a Dream

The Great Creation
The idea that reality is a projection of the mind

Now imagine that the universe is something similar, created by a very great mind. Everything we feel and experience, such as energy and matter, are part of this great dream.

The power of thoughts

Our Super Power
The influence that our thoughts have on our life.

Notice that your thoughts are very powerful. Look, when you think about something you want to accomplish, like learning to ride a bike,

Practice and
Faith

Persistence and Growth
The importance of practice and faith in yourself.

your mind starts working on it. It may be difficult at first, but if you keep practicing and believing in yourself, you will eventually get there.

The Influence of Thoughts

The Impact of Beliefs
How our beliefs can shape our actions and achievements

This shows how your thoughts can influence what you do and what you can achieve.

The power of imagination

Imagination and creativity
The power of creativity and self-observation in our lives.

All human beings also have an immense power called imagination, creativity and self-observation.

An Adventure in the Mind

Escaping Anxiety
The ability to transform anxiety through imagination.

Look at this example: when you are in a place waiting and there is a very long line, your mind begins to get impatient, you close your eyes and begin to imagine that you are on an adventure, like exploring an island full of treasures, your mind will take you to that place exciting and anxiety will disappear,

The Key of Knowledge

Knowledge as a Key
The understanding that knowledge can open new doors

Even if you are physically in the same place, your mind can make you feel happy and excited. This shows how the mind can change our experience of the world.

Positive Thinking

Optimism and Confidence
The importance of maintaining a positive attitude

The magical key to knowledge is when you understand that the universe is like a big idea in your mind. You can learn to use that to improve your life.

Moving towards Knowledge

The Path of Knowledge
The connection between the mind and personal growth

It's like having a magic key that opens doors for you. If you know how to be positive and confident, you can think more optimistically and see how that improves your daily life.

The Creative Mind

Influence of Our Thoughts
The relevance of being aware of our thoughts.

When you understand
that everything is mental,
you are advancing on
your path to knowledge.
So remember: your
thoughts are powerful
and can help you create
the life you want!

Creating the Life You Want

Creating Your Future
The power of the mind to manifest our desires

—In conclusion, everything we see and experience in the world is part of the powerful mind of the creator of all things. Our thoughts are very important as they can influence our actions and how we live our lives.

Present Awareness

Present Moment
Awareness
The relevance of living in the here and now

By understanding that everything is mental, we can learn to be more positive and achieve our dreams. Remember: your thoughts have the power to create the life you want. Use this magic! It is at your disposal.

Self-Observation

Know Yourself
The importance of self-reflection in personal growth.

Sofía asked Silfo what is Self-Observation? to which Silfo answered with great joy: it is the ability of human beings to pay attention to their thoughts and feelings.

Facing Fear

Courage in the face of Fear
The importance of facing our fears with courage.

Self-observation will help you to always be aware of the present moment and will help you prevent negative thoughts from hurting you.

Disintegrating Fear

Eliminating Negative Thoughts

The power of asking for help to overcome difficult thoughts

Sofía asked Silfo what happens if I have an ugly thought and it scares me. Silfo answered: if this happens to you, observe the thought, you have to be brave, even if you feel afraid, at that moment you ask the great architect of the universe, the divine part that is within you, to disintegrate that thought.

The Three Keys to Awakening Consciousness

Keys to Consciousness
The importance of self-observation in self-knowledge.

Silfo recommended that Sofía practice self-observation from moment to moment, be aware of the Here and Now and revealed to her the three keys to awakening consciousness: Who I am, where I am and what I am doing. Become aware!

A valuable gift

Value what we learn
The value of all the teachings we receive in life

Exploring the World of Elementals

Exploration and Learning
Curiosity about the world and its purpose

Sofia was very excited about the teaching she was receiving and knew deep down that it was one of the most valuable gifts she would receive in her life.

After a brief silence, the Great Pavana entered, inviting Sofia to go out and see the rest of the town, and learn about the Elemental World of Air, its mission and what the goal is in human evolution.

The Time to Wake Up

Awaken to Reality
The transition between sleep and wakefulness

Soon a big bell rang and a soft voice told her: "Sofia, wake up, it's time to do homework."

Wake up with Joy

The Joy of Awakening
The happiness you feel when you return to reality

His body began to quickly fly towards his physical body. Sofia woke up with joy and great spirits,

Return to Dreams

The Connection with the Higher Worlds

The possibility of returning to the world of dreams and finding his friends

Sofia was certain that she could return to the world of dreams whenever she wanted, where her dear friends were waiting for her.

"Following this"

The Principle of Mentalism

"The Kybalion" states that "the All is Mind; the universe is mental." This means that the reality we perceive is a manifestation of the mind and that everything that exists is, in essence, a mental creation. This principle suggests that our thoughts and beliefs have significant power in shaping our experiences and reality.

Friends' Comments

"Wow! This story is amazing. I had never thought of the physical world as being like a dream. I loved the idea that my thoughts can make things happen. It's like having superpowers! When I think of something I want, like learning to play a new video game or doing a trick on my bike, I feel more motivated."

"Now I understand that if I believe in myself and stay positive, I can achieve it. I also like the part about imagination. Sometimes, when I'm bored, I close my eyes and imagine myself on cool adventures. It's awesome to know that my mind can make me feel happy and excited! I will try to think more positively and use my imagination to create amazing things. Thank you for sharing this!"